The ArtScroll Children's Holiday Series

(9)

Yaffa Ganz

LAG BA'OMER
AND TU BISHVAT
WITH BINA, BENNY AND CHAGGAI HAYONAH

Illustrated by Liat Benyaminy Ariel

Shalom! I'm Chaggai Hayonah — Chaggai the holiday dove.

Would you like to hear about ...
Two different holidays, two different seasons,
Different customs, different reasons?
In a way, both are the same.
Both use numbers for a name!

I bet Bina and Benny know which holidays I'm talking about ...

Bina was busy peeling a big, juicy orange and thinking.

"Lag Ba'Omer and Tu BiShvat are funny holidays," she said. "Neither day has any special prayers to say. There are no candles to light, no *kiddush* to make, no reading in the Torah. And neither day has a real name — only a number. Aren't they important holidays, Chaggai?"

Chaggai puffed himself up and preened a feather. "They most certainly are," he answered.

"How can they be important if there is nothing to do and no way to celebrate?" asked Benny.

"Of course there are things to do and ways to celebrate! Which things would you like to know about?"

"Everything!" said Bina and Benny together.

THE OMER HATENUFAH

"hat was the *Omer*, Chaggai?" asked Bina.

"What is *Sefiras Ha'Omer*?" asked Benny.

"What was Lag Ba'Omer?" both asked.

"Oh my! One question at a time, please! Let's begin at the beginning ... with the *Omer*.

"In the Land of Israel, crops are planted during the rainy, winter season. By the spring, the first grains are ripe and ready for the harvest. *Hashem* wanted to bless the produce of the fields, and He wanted us to be thankful for the harvest. He commanded us to bring the *Omer*. The *Omer* was an offering of the new barley crop — the first grain to ripen. It was called *Minchas Bikkurim* — the First Fruit Offering.

"On the second night of Pesach, messengers from the *Beis Din* went out to the fields. They cut down stalks of ripe barley, placed them in baskets, and brought them to the courtyard of the *Beis Hamikdash*. Everyone came to watch. The barley was softly beaten, parched in fire, dried, and ground into coarse flour. An *Omer* of flour — approximately four pounds worth — was then sifted through thirteen sieves and mixed with oil and frankincense, a sweet-smelling spice.

"The *Kohen* took the mixture and waved it in all four directions, to show that the entire world belongs to G–d. Then he waved it up and down, to show that G–d gives the rain from the sky and the dew from the earth. That's why it's called *Omer Hatenufah* — the *Omer* of Waving."

"That's the same reason we have for waving the *lulav* and *esrog* on Succos!" said Benny.

"I'm glad you remember!" said Chaggai. "A small part of the *Omer* was burnt on the Altar and the rest was eaten by the *Kohanim.* After the *Omer* was brought, the people were allowed to eat the grain from all of the new crops — wheat, barley, spelt, rye and oats."

ERETZ YISRAEL AND
THE BEIS HAMIKDASH

"Can we still bring the *Omer*?" asked Benny.

"Oh no!" said Chaggai. "The *Omer* can only be brought to the *Beis Hamikdash*, in *Eretz Yisrael*."

"Oh well, I guess that's another mitzvah we'll have

to wait for," sighed Benny. "We really need the *Beis Hamikdash*. There are so many things we can't do without it."

"That's true. And the *Omer* is a special *mitzvah* for *Eretz Yisrael*. The Torah says ...

"... when you come into the Land that I give you and you reap its harvest, you shall bring an *Omer* from your first harvest to the *Kohen*. (*Vayikra* 23:10)

"The *Omer* was a way of saying thank you to G–d Who blesses the Land and its produce. And it reminded the people that even with all of their hard work, they still need *Hashem* to help them."

All this talking about barley and wheat and blessings is making me hungry! Maybe I'll try some barley seed for a change. I bet it's tasty ...

SEFIRAS HA'OMER

"What is *Sefiras Ha'Omer*?" asked Benny.

"It's the Counting of the *Omer,* and it's one of the 613 *mitzvos* in the Torah. We are commanded to count forty-nine days, seven full weeks, from the day we bring the *Omer* on the second day of Pesach, until the holiday of Shavuos, fifty days later."

"Who counts the forty-nine days?" asked Bina.

"You do, Benny does, we all do!" answered Chaggai. "Each evening we make a *berachah* and count a day. When we begin counting, it's Pesach, the time G–d took us out of Egypt. When we finish counting, it's Shavuos and *Z'man Mattan Toraseinu* — the time we received the Torah at Mount Sinai. So you see, *Sefiras Ha'Omer* is a very special time. It's seven weeks of waiting for the Torah, seven weeks when we try to turn ourselves into better people who *deserve* the Torah."

"I'm glad we can still count the days of the *Omer,* even if we can't bring the *Omer* itself," said Bina.

"And I'm glad we have forty-nine days to prepare, so we'll be ready for *Mattan Torah*!" said Benny.

LAG BA'OMER

"ou still haven't explained what Lag Ba'Omer means," said Benny.

"That's easy," said Bina, "*Lamed* equals the number thirty and *gimmel* equals three. Together, the two letters add up to thirty-three and that's exactly what Lag Ba'Omer is — the thirty-third day in the counting of the *Omer*. It falls on the eighteenth day in the month of *Iyar*."

"I know that, but why is it a holiday?" asked Benny.

"That is a long tale to tell," sighed the Dove. He fluffed his feathers and shook his head. "Come sit down and I'll tell you about it.

RABBI AKIVA

"After the destruction of the Second *Beis Hamikdash*, the Romans ruled the Land of Israel with an iron fist. Even though they forbade the Jews to learn the Torah or to keep its laws, the Jews continued to study and do *mitzvos*."

"Then a terrible plague spread through the land. It happened during the days of the *Omer*. Twenty-four thousand of Rabbi Akiva's students died between Pesach and Shavuos. Ever since then, the days of the *Omer* are a period of mourning. The rabbis said we may not make weddings, listen to music, celebrate, or cut our hair during these days.

"The plague lasted for thirty-three days. On Lag Ba'Omer — the 33rd day in the *Omer* — no one died. That's why Lag Ba'Omer was declared a day of rejoicing."

"That's awful!" cried Bina. "Why did so many of Rabbi Akiva's students die? Why did G–d let the plague spread?"

"The rabbis said they died because they did not treat each other with enough honor and respect. The Torah commands us: וְאָהַבְתָּ לְרֵעֲךָ כָּמוֹךָ —*You shall love your neighbor as you love yourself.* This is one of the most important laws in the Torah. But they were not careful enough with this *mitzvah.*

"When the plague ended, Rabbi Akiva had only five students left. He started teaching Torah and opening new yeshivos again. *Am Yisrael* continued to study the Torah and to fulfill the *mitzvos.* Even the mighty Roman Empire was not strong enough to separate the Jewish people from the Torah."

❖   ❖   ❖

"Wasn't Rabbi Akiva afraid? How could he teach Torah if the Romans were always watching?"

"Afraid? No, Rabbi Akiva was never afraid. Even when he was finally caught and imprisoned, he never stopped teaching. Until the day he died, he fought the Romans with his own fiery weapon — the flaming words of the Torah. Even though the Romans killed him, he won the war."

"I wish I could have been one of Rabbi Akiva's students," said Benny wistfully.

"You are," said Chaggai. "All Jews everywhere are his students. If it weren't for Rabbi Akiva, the Torah would have been forgotten. Rabbi Akiva saved the Torah for the Jewish people."

RABBI SHIMON BAR YOCHAI

"W hat about Rabbi Shimon bar Yochai? Lag Ba'Omer is about him, too!" said Bina.

"Of course it is!" answered Chaggai. "Rabbi Shimon bar Yochai was a student of Rabbi Akiva. And just like his teacher, he, too, had to hide from the Romans to study the Torah. Rabbi Shimon and his son Elazar hid in a cave in Peki'in, high in the mountains of the Galil. For thirteen years they sat and studied in the cave. They ate fruit from a carob tree and drank water from a small stream that G–d made flow outside the cave. Only after the Roman Emperor died were Rabbi Shimon and Rabbi Elazar able to come out of hiding.

"Rabbi Shimon died on the eighteenth of *Iyar*, which is Lag Ba'Omer. That day, he revealed much of the secret wisdom of the Torah to his students. It was a long, miraculous day, because the sun did not set in the sky until Rabbi Shimon finished teaching. It was a day filled with great light and joy."

"Isn't it amazing?" said Bina. "Rabbi Akiva's students did not die on Lag Ba'Omer, and years later, on Lag Ba'Omer, a student of Rabbi Akiva brought new light and Torah to the world!"

CELEBRATING LAG BA'OMER

ut Bina still looked troubled.

"Chaggai," she asked, "what do we *do* on Lag Ba'Omer if there are no special prayers, no *kiddush*, no wine, no blessings over candles, no reading in the Torah, no special *mitzvos*?"

"What do you mean what do we do? We rejoice! We are happy to have the Torah and to be part of such a wonderful nation!"

"We take haircuts," said Benny, looking at his long hair. "I haven't had a haircut since Erev Pesach! Lots of little boys have their first haircut on Lag Ba'Omer."

"We go to weddings," said Bina thoughtfully, "Our cousins Motti and Ilana and getting married on Lag Ba'Omer."

"We have picnics, outings and hikes! That's the part I like best," said Chaggai. "Where there are lots of trees and grass and good seeds to eat."

"In *Eretz Yisrael*," said Chaggai, "thousands of people go up to Meiron, to the graves of Rabbi Shimon and his son Rabbi Elazar. They light a huge bonfire and dance and sing and study the *Zohar*, the book of Torah wisdom that Rabbi Shimon wrote."

"They make bonfires all over Eretz Yisrael. I read about it," said Benny. "But the biggest bonfire of all is in Meiron."

"I think the bonfires are also in honor of Rabbi Akiva," said Bina. "You told us Rabbi Akiva fought the Romans and won the war with his own *fiery* weapon — the flaming words of the Torah!"

TU BISHVAT

"When does a new year begin before the old year is over?" asked Benny.

"That's easy," answered Bina. "Tu BiShvat is the Rosh Hashanah La'Ilanos — the beginning of the year for trees. And it comes in the month of Shvat, which is the eleventh month of the year after Nissan. You know that!"

"I know I know it. I was just trying to see if *you* know it too! But I wonder why trees need a New Year. What's new about it?"

"I don't know," said Bina. "Let's ask Chaggai."

Chaggai was examining the buds of the apricot tree in the garden.

"Can you come down, Chaggai? We need you," called Benny.

"The trees are doing very well up here," answered the Dove. "They're almost ready for Tu BiShvat. Soon they'll be covered with leaves."

"That's just what we wanted to talk to you about — trees! Why do trees need a Rosh Hashanah? They aren't people."

"They may not be people, but they happen to be very important. Any bird can tell you that! And many important things have a Rosh Hashanah. In fact, there are *four* different Rosh Hashanahs — New Years — in the year.

 "NISSAN begins a new year for counting the reign of the kings of Israel ...

ELUL begins a new year for tithing animals ...

 TISHREI begins a new year for people ...

TU BiShvat begins a new year for trees and for tithing their fruit ..."

ROSH HASHANAH LA'ILANOS

"Tu BiShvat is a funny name for a New Year. It doesn't even begin at the beginning of the month," said Benny.

"Of course not," answered Chaggai. "It comes in the middle of the month, on the fifteenth day of Shvat. The letters Tes and Vav — Tu — equal fifteen."

"Why can't trees have the same New Year people have?"

"Because they have different needs! In *Eretz Yisrael*, it rains in the winter, and by Tu BiShvat most of the rain has fallen. The soil is moist, the sap is rising in the trees, the branches are beginning to bud and even though it's still cold, spring is on its way. Soon everything will turn green and bloom.

"Just as Rosh Hashanah is a Day of Judgment for people, Tu BiShvat is a Day of Judgment for trees. A new tree-year is beginning and G–d will decide which trees will grow, which will die; which will be strong and healthy and give good fruit, and which will be sickly or weak."

"You make trees sound just like people," said Benny.

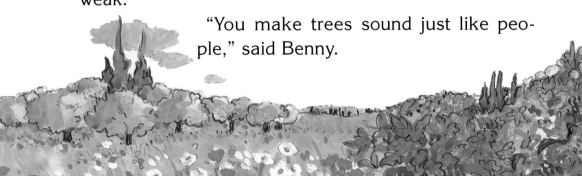

"Trees aren't people, but people are compared to trees," said Chaggai. "A person is compared to *a tree of the field* — כִּי הָאָדָם עֵץ הַשָּׂדֶה."

"How do the trees celebrate their Rosh Hashanah?" asked Bina. "They can't pray, can they?"

"Not that I know of," answered Chaggai. "But *we* celebrate and *we* pray. Tu BiShvat is a weekday Rosh Hashanah — a happy, joyful day. It's the perfect time to ask *Hashem* to grow a beautiful *esrog* for us to use on the holiday of Succos."

"What else do we do on Tu BiShvat besides ask for an *esrog*?"

"We eat, of course! Not just our everyday fish and chicken and meat, but fruit! Especially new fruit, so we can make the blessing *Shehecheyanu.* And especially new fruit from *Eretz Yisrael.*"

"Isn't regular fruit from the supermarket good enough?" asked Benny.

"Ah ...," sighed the dove, "there is no comparison between supermarket fruit and fruit from the Land of Israel! The fruit of *Eretz Yisrael* is unlike any other. Here, have a raisin and I'll tell you about it ..."

SHIVAS HAMINIM — THE SEVEN FRUITS

Chaggai sat on a low branch of the apricot tree. He chewed on a raisin and thought a while before he began to speak.

"Tu BiShvat is a joyful day because on the 15th of Shvat G–d renews the strength of the soil of *Eretz Yisrael*. And when the soil is strong and healthy, *Eretz Yisrael* becomes a Land Flowing with Milk and Honey. It produces wonderful fruit — especially the *Shivas HaMinim* — the Seven Fruits blessed by G–d with a special Holy Land blessing. They are ...

wheat and barley,

grape, figs and pomegranates,

olives and dates."

"And when the Land produces its fruit, the Jewish people rejoice and are happy," said Bina.

"And when the Jewish people are happy, they thank *Hashem* and bless Him," said Benny.

"And when they bless *Hashem, Hashem* blesses them in return!" ended Chaggai. "That's exactly what we say in the *Bircas Hamazon* after we eat:

"You shall eat and be satisfied and bless *Hashem* your G–d for the good Land which He gave you!"

❖ ❖ ❖

"Did you get everything you need for Tu BiShvat?" asked Benny.

"I think so," said Bina. "I couldn't find fresh grapes from Israel, but I bought raisins. Chaggai said dried fruits are just as good as fresh ones. And Abba will bring wine. And I have dates, figs, pomegranates and olives. Imma is baking carob cookies."

"Look, Bina! It's snowing outside! Spring seems pretty far away, doesn't it?"

"It seems far away here, but with all this fruit, I can almost smell the blossoms in *Eretz Yisrael*!"

A TIME FOR TREES

"**H**ere's a picture of the trees our class planted in *Eretz Yisrael*. I think of them every Tu BiShvat. I hope they will grow well this year. Some of those trees must be pretty big by now. I can't wait to see them!"

Chaggai looked at the picture Benny was holding. "I'm sure they've grown into splendid trees, Benny. Shall I ask a few of my dove-cousins from Israel to find them and take a look for you?"

"No, thank you," said Benny. "I'm saving my money and *b'ezras Hashem,* as soon as I have enough for a plane ticket, I'll go take a look myself. I want to plant a tree by myself, too."

"Let's start eating some of that fruit," said Bina, "or else it may begin to sprout! And who knows ... maybe next year, we'll plant and eat in *Eretz Yisrael*!"

I *love* Tu BiShvat! It's a real bird holiday!

Did you know that ...

... before *Hashem* created Adam He planted *Gan Eden* — the Garden of Eden?

"And G–d planted a garden eastward of Eden and He put the man whom He had created there."

... Adam was commanded to work in the Garden of Eden?

"And G–d took Man and placed him in Gan Eden to cultivate it and to guard it."

... Jewish people were told to plant fruit trees as soon as they entered the Land of Israel?

"When you come into the Land, you shall plant fruit trees ..."

... long ago in *Eretz Yisrael*, when a child was born, the parents planted a tree? Then, when the children grew up and were married, branches from their trees were used to make their wedding canopy.

... today Tu BiShvat has become a favorite day for planting trees in the Land of Israel?

TU BISHVAT & LAG BA'OMER

"ven though Lag Ba'Omer and Tu BiShvat are two separate holidays," said Chaggai, "I think there is something very important they both share. Do you know what it is?"

Chaggai fluttered his wings and waited for an answer.

"We said both days use numbers for names, each is one day long, and there are no special prayers on either day," said Bina. "I can't think of anything else."

"Neither can I," agreed Benny.

"What about the doves?" Chaggai fluttered his wings again.

"The doves?" Benny and Bina looked confused.

"Yes, of course. Tu BiShvat and Lag Ba'Omer are perfect dove holidays! Doves particularly appreciate trees and of course we always love a few good *Omer*-barley grains to eat during the harvest. I wonder why the rabbis didn't mention us."

"You're always thinking about doves!" said Bina.

Chaggai puffed himself up. "Well, doves *are* pretty important birds, you know! They're mentioned many times in the Torah. Even the Jewish people are compared to doves!"

"I agree!" laughed Bina.

"Doves *are* important birds and the world is their garden where each and every flower and tree, each

and every fruit and grain, has its own special *mitzvah* and its own perfect place."

"That," said Chaggai, "is because *Hashem* is the perfect Master Gardener!

"May your days be brimming with Torah and your fields be full of fruits and grains, flowers and trees!

"May you plant and harvest, study and learn, celebrate and bring the *Omer* next year to the *Beis Hamikdash*, in the Land of Israel!

"Have a happy Tu BiShvat and a lovely Lag Ba'Omer!"

GLOSSARY

Beis Din — A Rabbinical Court; here, the High Court in Jerusalem

Beis Hamikdash — the Holy Temple in Jerusalem

b'ezras Hashem — with the help of G–d

Bircas Hamazon — prayer after eating a meal with bread

Eretz Yisrael — the land of Israel

Galil — the Galilee; the northern part of Israel

Hashem — G–d

Iyar — the second month in the Hebrew year

kiddush — the special blessing over wine on Shabbos and festival meals

Kohen / Kohanim — descendants of Aaron, priests in the Holy Temple

Mattan Torah — the Giving of the Torah

mitzvah / mitzvos — commandment(s) of the Torah

Pesach — the holiday of Passover

Rosh Hashanah — the New Year

Shavuos — the Holiday of Weeks, celebrating our receiving the Torah

Shvat — the eleventh month in the Hebrew year

Succos — the Holiday of Booths